Willow Moon Publishing

Willow Moon Publishing, 108 Saint Thomas Road, Lancaster, PA 17601,willow-moon-publishing.com

Cataloging Data
Brewer Gant, Kirsten, The Matter of the May Mouse/ by Kirsten Brewer Gant; illustrations by A Fomin.
Summary: The Matter of the May Mouse teaches that greatness can come in any size. Hardcover ISBN:
978-1-948256-27-8 {1. Juvenile Fiction/General. 2. Juvenile Fiction/Animals / Mice, Hamsters, Guinea
Pigs, Squirrels, etc. 3. Juvenile Fiction/Family / General 4. Stories in rhyme}

The Matter of the May Mouse

Written by
Kirsten
Brewer Gant

Illustrated by
A. Fomin

This is for Greta and all the great big things that come in teeny, tiny packages.

Beneath a great big house,

in a wee little mouse-hole,

Or so the Mouse legends say

Live Papa Mouse, Mama Mouse,

big sisters- April, June, and July,

And of course, who could forget, little May.

Now May Mouse was a tiny little mouse,

And an itty bitty mouse was May,

With large floppy ears, and a great big smile,

And hair of the softest gray.

And the Mouse Family loved their May Mouse so dearly

But that love turned to worry each day

About why their May Mouse just didn't seem to grow,

And if teeny tiny she would stay.

"Mice are small as a rule," Papa Mouse would say,

"But a mouse itty bitty

won't do!"

"How can a teeny mouse survive in this world?" said Mama,

"Just what can become of you?"

And in that mouse-hole, the Mouse family had ideas

On how to make their May Mouse big.

Everyday her family would offer suggestions

Of how to make May grow to the size of a fig.

"You must nibble more cheese!" bossed big sister April.

"No," cried June, "More stretching is what May should do!"

"Try dreaming bigger dreams," offered July shyly.

"Oh May, we all feel so sorry for you!"

And through all this advice and worry

Little May never let herself get down,

She went about her day, playing and laughing,

Searching for treasures with nary a frown.

You see, little May Mouse didn't mind being small,

She didn't mind it at all,

She knew her smallness was what made her special,

Her smallness was a gift, after all.

One day, the Mouse family discovered a treasure,

Deep within the wall.

It was a spool of golden yarn, dropped by the big house people,

And to the Mouse Family, finders-keepers is law!

"Oh what we could do with that golden yarn," said Mama,

"But it's just out of our reach."

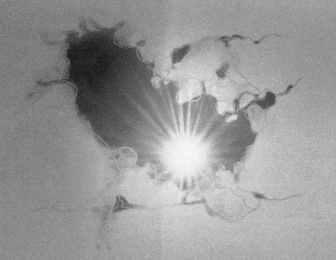

"We could make golden dresses!" cried April. "Golden hats!" said June.

"Or golden suits to wear to the beach!"

And Papa Mouse could reach out and barely touch

With his great big Papa Mouse paw,

That golden yarn, so soft and pretty

Deep within the wall.

But try as he might he just could not

Pull that golden thread out

of the wall,

"Either my arm's too big or the hole's too small," said Papa,

"To reach that yarn at all!"

"But what about me?" whispered May Mouse,

Smiling her widest smile,

"I can fit in that hole and reach the thread," she said,

And everyone was quiet for awhile.

"Might as well try," said Mama Mouse.

"I don't see what it would harm."

And May Mouse scurried with ease right through that hole,

And WHOOSH, out came the yarn!

"She did it!" cried June, as the Mouse Family smiled

At their new golden treasure found.

They threw little May on their proud mouse shoulders,

And in happy circles they danced around!

May put her little mouse feet back on the floor

And said with solemn eyes,

"I hope now you'll remember

That a mouse's value is not about her size.

I can laugh and dance, and find treasures

And eat cheese, even though I'm small.

I'm an important mouse, just like you.

My smallness doesn't matter at all."

And the Mouse family hugged little May tight

And wiped tears from their eyes,

And never again did they worry about May.

They knew she was her perfect size.

About the Author

Kirsten Brewer Gant lives in the Atlanta suburbs with one still-sweet teenager, a set of rambunctious triplets, and one mangy dog. When Kirsten is not chasing aforementioned kids and dog, she spends her time taxiing small bodies around creation, hunting for lost shoes and overselling her mediocre cooking to her family.

If all those tasks are completed, she enjoys reading, taking barre classes, hiking, and writing the occasional article or children's book.

Kirsten holds a BA in Creative Writing from Florida State University and a Masters of Mass Communication from The University of Georgia, which pretty much just means she is awesome at diagramming sentences.

Seriously, if you want an A on your 5th grade English homework, give her a ring (but not right now because one of the triplets just flushed it down the commode).

About the Illustrators

A&A Fomin, aka Alexander and Anna Fomin are family magicians from Russia. Every artist is a little bit of a Magician. Pushing the limits of the usual, they open the door to a fairy tale, a fantasy world familiar to us all beginning inchildhood.

They raise two wonderful daughters: Olga and Irina, love to travel and invent fairy-tale characters.

Their dream is to see and learn the cultural characteristics of as many countries as possible. They believe that love and support for each other is the most important thing that helps them in life.

They will be happy to ive you a tour of their fabulous worlds, you just need to do is ask!

CPSIA information can be obtained
at www.ICGtesting.com
Printed in the USA
BVHW091951061119
563113BV00004B/23/P

9 781948 256278